Wedding
Score

Wedding Score

AMANDA TERO

Wedding Score

© 2019 by Amanda Tero

Published by Amanda Tero
Decatur, MS 39327

All Scripture references taken from the King James Version. Public domain.

This novel is a work of fiction. The characters in this story are fictitious. Any resemblance to persons living or dead is coincidental.

ISBN: 978-1-942931-31-7

_____

Cover design by Amanda Tero
Images from
    www.pixabay.com
    www.shutterstock.com
Used by permission.

Formatted by Amanda Tero

For my oldest sister, Jessica

You were the first one of us to live through
these prolonged years of singleness.
Because I had you to look up to,
I was spared many of the struggles
that single girls face—such as
expecting to be married soon
after graduation. Thank you for being
a godly example to us younger sisters.
Your singleness is worth it.

One

The double doors swung open. I instantly ran my fingers over the piano keys with the exhilarating introduction of the Bridal Chorus. The audience moved with a gentle *swoosh* as everyone rose to their feet to watch Addison enter. I could barely see her through the throng of people, so I kept sneaking glances toward Harper, the groom. If I wasn't mistaken, that was a tear glistening in his eye as he gave his bride one of those million-dollar smiles. Addison and Uncle Bryan stepped to the front just as I reached the cadence.

Perfect timing. I'd take that. Even though I was used to lengthening or shortening this classic, I wasn't about to complain about well-timed synchronization. I leaned back as the preacher asked, "Who gives this bride to be married to this man?"

A few seconds later, while everyone bowed their heads for the opening prayer, I slipped from the piano bench to a chair that was closer to the wall. This was my prime wedding-watching spot. I had done it dozens of times and was prepared to do it again. From here, I could see the families of the bride and groom and watch their expressions. It gave a greater overview of the wedding than most guests received.

As soon as the preacher said "amen," my phone buzzed—almost as if the sender knew the timing. I discreetly glanced at the screen.

Meet for coffee when you're done?

Caiden. My cousin from Dad's side of the family.

I glanced around, wishing I was more like Mom, who saw the miracle in every wedding—and cried for almost every single one. I searched for her in the crowd. Sure enough, a gentle smile graced her face. I flicked my gaze back to my phone.

Sure... what's her name? ;)

It didn't take long for Caiden's reply to come in.

You know you just guess that each time for one-in-a-million chance you're right. JUST so you can "say so."

I bit back the smile. Yep. He knew me well. I sent an angel face emoji.

Caiden: You're not texting during a wedding again?

Another angel face reply.

Stephanie Lynn! Yo' mama's gonna tan yo' hide.

Ooh. Full name use here. I grinned as I slipped the phone into the invisible pocket of my black dress. I checked on Mom. No she wouldn't. She was wiping away tears now as the preacher was talking about the beauty of joining two individuals to make a new family. I gave a contented sigh and crossed my ankles. I had an easy repertoire for Addison's wedding. She wasn't a musician—hardly anyone on Mom's side was—so she had told me, "just do your thing." I was cool with that. But even though Addison didn't have a preference, Aunt Kim did. "All traditional." It may be a tad boring for my tastes, but it worked out. These pieces didn't require practice like the last wedding where the groom—not the bride—requested ten country love songs to be played for the prelude. Songs I didn't know, of course.

I jerked my attention back to the preacher. There had only been a short ceremony rehearsed. No unity candle— or sand, or three-knot rope—was being done. I didn't want to miss my cue to start "Wedding March" from *Midsummer Night's Dream.*

"You may now kiss your bride."

There it was. I slipped back onto the piano bench while the crowd cheered, and someone whistled. I kept playing while the bridal party and family exited, paused while the preacher made the reception announcement, then resumed playing various hymns and classical pieces while the crowd dwindled.

I left my binder and water bottle at the piano to grab later and trailed through the vacant auditorium. Happy chatter and laughter was my guide to the reception hall, even though without it, I knew my way fairly well around the church my cousins attended.

"Ah! Stephie. I was just about to go rescue you." Uncle Bryan winked at me as he pulled me into a hug. "Lovely job, as always."

"Thanks." I squeezed him back. "How does it feel to actually have a son now?" He often complained about being outnumbered with Aunt Kim and three daughters.

"Now to get two more," Uncle Bryan said. Though the way his eyes lingered after Addison made me think he wasn't in *too* much of a hurry to marry his other girls off. "I'm sure Brock won't complain if you take up the torch next, though."

I laughed lightly. "Dad's fine with me staying as I am a bit longer." As I stepped toward the food table, Uncle Bryan gave me that endearing smile and moved away to greet his other guests.

I had barely finished fixing my plate when Uncle Charlie sauntered up. "Great job, Steph."

"Thank you."

"This makes wedding number—what—that you've played for?"

Oh boy. I knew where this conversation was going. "Haven't counted, but it's the sixth this year." And it was only March.

"When will it be your turn to walk to the chorus, instead of playing it?"

Yep, there it was. Except, what he didn't know was that I was *not* intending to walk to the Bridal Chorus. I was going to choose something… less traditional. Something that I hadn't heard six hundred times.

Uncle Charlie gave me a friendly nudge, and I kept a tight grip on my plate to keep the food from sliding off. "Oh, I don't know." I lifted my shoulder in a carefree shrug. "Still waiting on God's timing." The pat answer came with ease. I'd only given it like every day for the past ten years.

"Just you wait. Some guy is out there and will totally sweep you off your feet."

I grinned. "Sure." I nodded toward the drink fountain. "Gonna grab me some punch. Do you want some?"

"Nah, thanks though, hon." He patted his stomach. "Gotta watch that blood sugar."

We laughed, then I slipped away to fill a punch cup. I drank the full serving of punch in one unladylike guzzle. I should probably watch my blood sugar too. After all, I was nearing thirty. I ignored that thought and filled my cup again before moving away. Most people got sparkly-eyed for the wedding cake. Me? I was totally a punch-girl. At least, for those weddings where I knew beyond a doubt that the punch wasn't spiked.

I found a quiet place by the wall to eat and watch the crowd—my family, mostly. Mom's family was a decent size. She had one sister, two brothers. Each family averaged three kids—though the balance was slightly off. I had only one sister, Uncle Bryan three daughters, Aunt Theresa a son, then Uncle Charlie held the weight of half the grandkids with his six. Since I was an ancient, six years older than any of the other cousins, I was closer to the aunts than the kids.

I slipped my phone out of my pocket and texted Caiden, *When is it socially polite to leave?*

I held the phone loosely in my hand as I finished eating. Five minutes passed, and he still didn't reply. Well, then. I threw my plate away and gave polite smiles and exchanged chit-chat with a few people. My phone buzzed. I glanced at it as I wove around the guests.

Aren't you supposed to be the wedding expert? You know, "Always the pianist, never the bride...?"

Oh man. If he were present, I'd so punch him. Playfully, of course. And he knew that. He knew just how to goad for a reaction. It was part of the camaraderie we'd always had growing up together, being the only two children born on Dad's side until my younger sister came along ten years later.

The crowd shifted, and I put away my phone so I could watch Addison and Harper smear cake on each other's faces. I glanced at my watch. A half hour tops and we'd be blowing bubbles at the happy couple as they departed. Then I'd meet Caiden at whichever coffee shop he chose and offer that punch in person.

Two

"Caramel frappe for you, real coffee for me." Caiden didn't have to speak loudly for me to hear him as I entered the coffee shop. It was one of the quiet ones—which was perfect for an after-wedding adrenaline crash.

"Guess that diffuses my anger," I commented as I slid onto the barstool beside him. "Do we have to sit with this scenery?" I nodded toward the big window in front of us, facing a busy highway.

Caiden grumbled, but he swung off the barstool and motioned toward a booth. We settled across from each other and he leaned forward to whisper, "Better view here?" He straightened and struck a pose.

I shook my head as I grinned. If we weren't cousins, I would have definitely had a crush on him as a teen. Short-cropped dark hair, a slight grunge instead of a full-fledged beard—well, that hadn't been there as a teen—and a well-built frame that boasted of Caiden's commitment to the gym.

"Any prospects?" he asked.

"Huh?" I took a sip of the frappe.

"You know…" He wiggled his eyebrows at me. "If not, the barista here is pretty nice." He tilted his head to the guy behind the counter.

I sneaked a glance at him then glared at Caiden. "He's like a decade younger than me!"

"Nah, he's definitely eighteen."

"Whatever. *Almost* a decade younger than me." I noticed that Caiden still hadn't taken a drink of his black coffee. And his fingers were suspiciously white from clutching the cup. "So…" I struck my best innocent look. "What's her name?"

Caiden let out a whoosh of air and a goofy grin stretched across his face.

No. Way. I put my frappe to my lips but didn't dare drink any. I'd be sure to choke as soon as Caiden spilled the beans.

"Wanna guess?"

I gave up any pretense of sipping coffee and set it down. "For real?"

He didn't say anything. Just sat there, stone-faced.

"I mean…" My words tripped over each other. "I've got a good half dozen girls I *could* guess. Maybe one or two I'd actually be serious about. And then there are a few friends that you have that I don't know about." Well, that last comment was a ploy. I knew everyone Caiden hung around. He couldn't keep a secret from me to save his life.

"Guess then."

"Caiden! No. I'd be wrong." And *that* would be embarrassing. Which is probably exactly what he wanted.

"Rachel."

Funny how one word could sound like an explosion of fireworks when uttered softly. I couldn't school back my smile this time. "Rachel as in Rachel Wall? The pastor's daughter?" The preacher that I had just heard officiate my *other* cousin's wedding? Goodness. Rachel had probably been there too, but I didn't even think to look for her. Weird, how life crossed paths like that.

A hint of red framed Caiden's face. He actually dared to drink some coffee for the first time since we had started talking.

"So…?" I gestured for more info.

Caiden shrugged. "That's about it."

I flattened my hands on the table. "That is *not* about it, Caiden James. Did you ask her out? Did you *go* out?"

"Thursday night. And, I mean, we hung out some Wednesday night after Bible study."

Right. They both attended the same Bible study at college—he as a grad student, Rachel as undergrad. My heart deflated just a little as he launched into his excited monologue. He'd been out with her *twice* and this was the first he told me about it? Maybe he could keep more secrets than I credited him. I brushed past the thought and focused on his story.

"Her dad's cool with it. I met with him last night."

"Wait. Like… after he just spent two hours at wedding rehearsal?" I gaped at Caiden.

Caiden flung his hands in the air. "He offered. I mean, we'd been talking before I asked Rachel out. But he just wanted to sit and chat. He's a great guy. I was nervous as all get-out though." The way his hands twitched while he spoke, I almost thought he was nervous *now* in front of me—someone who could remember when he was born.

"Anyway, yeah, I wanted to tell you in person. See your reaction, you know." He couldn't keep that silly grin off his face. And I couldn't help but smile.

I took a sip of my frappe and let the flavors swirl in my mouth just one second.

"So now, all I have to do is find you a guy, then we can go on double dates."

I gasped then choked as the frappe went down the wrong way. Caiden offered me a napkin, but his smirk indicated he wasn't exactly sorry.

As soon as I could speak, I shook my head. "That was downright mean."

He just grinned.

"What's up with all these couples who think they're responsible to find a partner for all the singles out there just because *they* have someone?"

He crossed his arms and smiled.

"C'mon, Caid. *You* even harped on that subject, too. I can list the girls that you were match—"

"Yeah, that was then."

"Don't *even* start." Though I said it lightly and in jest, my heart tripped.

Caiden gave me a slow, conspiratorial wink. "Gotcha."

I kicked him under the table and he mock-howled.

My phone buzzed and I glanced down at it. My other best friend's name showed up in a text.

Livvy: I need to talk.

I frowned. Usually she wasn't quite so blunt.

Livvy: Soon? Please.

I waved my phone at Caiden. "Uh, it's Livvy. I think something's going on." Could it be her mom's last doctor's appointment? Maybe her dad had lost his job. Or she lost hers. Things had been shaky at work for her lately.

"Sure, I've got plans anyway." He tried to give a lackadaisical grin, but it turned into a full-fledged smile.

"Oh boy, you're smitten. Bitten bad."

"She's really great, Steph."

"And I'm really glad. You *need* the absolutely best person to put up with your mess."

"Hey now!" He clutched at his heart. "That hit me. Right here."

"Mhm."

We stood and I gave him a quick hug.

"Thanks for telling me in person. I'm really excited for you. Keep me updated!"

"You know I will."

He held the door open for me to exit the coffee shop. As soon as I was in the car, I put in a call to Livvy. The ringing stopped and things were muffled.

"Hey, Livvy?"

She sucked in what sounded like a sob. "Can you come over?"

I cranked my car. "Yeah. I'm actually in town right now. Be there in five."

She clicked off without saying anything else and worry flooded me.

Three

J sat on the bed, my arms around Livvy as she sobbed. She had greeted me with one word then cried.

"Jake."

Oh boy. There were dozens of questions that I wanted to ask, but now that I knew no one was dying or losing their livelihood, my heart had stopped its wild racing. This was just Livvy-drama with her boyfriend. Not that I took that lightly, but Livvy was the one who would cry when she dropped her doll face-down on the ground as a kid. I needed more details before I joined her tears. As it was, I just waited. Rubbed her back. Let her cry it out.

It was at least ten minutes before she sat back, blew her nose, and gave a half-laugh. "I look terrible."

I gave her a half-grin. "I think I've seen you worse."

"Thanks? I think?"

I shifted on the mattress. "So… what's up with you and Jake?"

Tears welled in her eyes and dripped down her cheeks. She didn't even move to wipe them away. "It's over."

She could have struck me with a sledgehammer; it would have had the same impact. "Over? Like *over*-over? Or just… kinda over?"

Now, she wiped at her tears, which were falling faster.

Okay, my reaction could have been gentler. I leaned closer. *Lord, give me wisdom to know what to say.* I tried to make my voice as tender and controlled as I could when in reality I wanted to screech. "What happened? I mean, I knew things were going kinda rough, but…" I shook myself. Okay, that probably wasn't God speaking through me, the way the shock came out in my voice. And it wouldn't help matters any.

She shrugged. "Nothing? Everything?"

Well that was helpful. I waited, not sure what questions to even ask. Last I heard, they were taking things slower—not quite a break, but almost a break. It had started when Jake had accepted a new job three states over without talking to Livvy first. Then, she had refused to entertain the thought of moving that far away from her parents if they did get married. But I thought they had worked all of that out. Livvy had agreed that Jake had been right to accept the job and start as soon as he was finished with his master's degree in May.

Livvy sucked in a shuddering breath. "So… we both just kinda have a lot we need to personally work through. Him with his family and job and stuff. Me with…" She crumpled the tissue in her hands. "I don't know. Just spiritual stuff. We didn't argue or explode or anything. Exactly…"

She had probably just cried, poor thing. Though, it was likely that Jake was feeling a lot of emotions, too. He was a great guy—didn't pretend to not feel when he did feel. They were both great people. Which was why this break-up confused me.

"Just, neither of us had a peace about moving forward. His parents weren't sure about him getting married right after graduating and we want their full blessing."

I glanced down at her left hand. No promise ring. Now, the tears stung the backs of my eyes and my throat went dry. They hadn't been engaged—Livvy had always insisted on a short engagement—but they were serious about this relationship heading toward marriage and were talking as if they were getting married. I did know that Jake and Livvy prayed about practically everything. It just didn't make this news any easier to swallow.

"I guess we knew it was coming. His parents have been asking him to push back thoughts of marriage until he was established. And then… I… just had a hard time supporting him in his decisions. Which isn't right if I'm going to be married to him."

I reached forward and patted her knee. She had taken great strides over the last few years with not leaning on her emotions, but I could tell she was battling them hard right now.

"I know it's our life to live, but the Bible says for children to honor their parents. We talked to our pastor and my parents. It's totally untraditional in today's world to let parents be involved in our relationship, but Jake and

I feel that maybe his parents are right and we need to step back. For now. Hopefully."

Leave it to Livvy to have her life chorded with a full ensemble of problems.

"But I don't really wanna talk about it."

I was cool with that. "Okay, we don't have to."

Silence hung in the air, but it wasn't a comfortable silence. It was threaded with tension. Like when you end a piece of music on a dissonant chord and the notes just hang there, unresolved and unsettling. My mind shuffled the list of verses I could share as comfort. Those about trusting in the Lord. Seeking the Lord. Waiting on the Lord. But she hadn't exactly asked for my opinion or comfort. She just wanted me here. So I stayed still and waited.

Finally, she drew her knees up and hugged them. "I guess I knew this was coming. It had to."

Well, *I* didn't see it coming. I ventured, "It sounds like the right decision." I wasn't fully convinced about it, but I just had to trust that if they were both seeking God, then He would guide them.

"I know… but why does it have to be *so hard?*" And the waterworks sprung again.

I waited, and in a minute they stopped.

"Okay, I'm done crying. I think." She dabbed her eyes with another tissue.

Good. I didn't dare say it out loud. We were polar opposites, but I knew my boundaries. I did feel sorry for her, but… it was more mixed with confusion. This was totally not what I expected to hear when she had texted me earlier.

"So, how was your day?"

Hmm… a wedding and my other best friend with his head in the clouds over his girlfriend? Yeah, I didn't think those would be topics she'd want to pursue right now. I chose a more neutral topic. "Have you been to that new coffee shop downtown? Java Press, I think. Caiden and I met there. Their caramel frappe is pretty amazing."

A wobbly smile graced Livvy's lips. "I'll have to try it on my way home from work Monday."

"Or we could just plan to meet up there sometime." Even if it was thirty minutes away from my home and a little inconvenient. But it had put a smile on her face for the moment. I'd do anything to keep things going that direction.

"Right, I know how your Mondays are."

She was right. For some reason, at the beginning of the school year, I had decided Mondays were a good day to add several private lessons *after* the group music lessons at a Christian academy. I wrinkled my nose at her. "But this week is spring break. Slow week."

"That's sweet, but I'll be fine." She drew in a huge breath. "At least, I think so."

I reached forward and grabbed her hand. "Yeah, you'll be fine."

We chit-chatted for a half hour, then she finally stood. "Thanks for coming by. I know you have to get ready for tomorrow. Don't want to keep you out late."

I rolled my eyes. "Seven o'clock isn't late."

"For one *your* age…"

I swatted her. That was the one thing about having best friends three and four years younger than me. They always took the chance to make me feel ancient at my twenty-seven years of age.

As soon as I was in the car and had backed away from Livvy's home, energy drained from me. What a *day*. Addison was married, Caiden got a girl, and Livvy lost her guy. Wow… Yeah, this definitely wasn't one of my best Saturdays.

Why does it always have to come in a flood? It was a prayer… kinda. I knew that nothing takes God by surprise, but sometimes I just wished He'd have given me a slight heads-up before dumping it all in my lap. I turned on some peppy Christian music to keep me awake as I drove out of town and toward the country outskirts where I lived. There was one last stop I'd have to make before calling it a night. I totally needed chocolate. And ice cream.

Four

*A*ddison, Bailey, Faith, Danielle, Lauren, Christine, Grace…

I jotted down the names of all my relatives and friends at whose weddings I had played. Uncle Charlie now had me curious. I kept good records, but had never counted the total number of weddings for which I had been pianist. I pulled out my ledger and added the list of clients to my friends and relatives. All the way back to when I was sixteen. I grinned as I remembered Becky's wedding. She was my second cousin—or first cousin once removed, however that went. I had been so nervous. That was another time when it seemed like life flooded me. I had just started teaching my first four piano students and was asked to play at my first wedding a month later. Now, looking back, it was amusing how much I had practiced. Today, eleven years later, I just had to brush up on pieces and they were ready. If someone asked me to play for a wedding the day before, I could whip it up. I *had* done it. On more than one occasion.

Speaking of practice... I really needed to run through the offertory number for tomorrow again. I could wing it, but I preferred actually knowing the order of chords I needed to transition between, and I totally didn't like being thrown-together on Sundays.

But first, I was going to get a headcount so I could offer it to Uncle Charlie next time I saw him. My pen slid over the names as I tallied up the numbers in my mind. One hundred sixty! That was a pretty impressive number, added up like that. Even if it did average only fifteen weddings a year. For a side job, it was perfect. I tossed the notebook aside and went to my piano.

The next day at church, I searched out Livvy as I played the first congregational. The piano facing the crowd of over one hundred people had its perks. Or its downfalls. I didn't see Livvy. And now I was worried. My phone was on the pew next to my Bible. I hadn't any qualms about texting during the wedding yesterday, but during church? That was only for emergencies—and this wasn't quite an emergency. As soon as everyone was dismissed from service, I pulled out my phone. A couple of missed messages flashed on my screen. There she was.

Not coming to church today. Have a headache. Don't worry. I won't make this a habit.

Well, apparently she did forewarn me, but I hadn't looked at my phone early enough. I waited until I was in my car before I replied.

Sorry about your headache. Been praying for you.
Livvy: Thanks, girlie.

I tossed my phone on the seat. Dad and Mom had taken my sister, Elise, on vacation during her spring break. Even though I no longer lived with them, in years past, I had still gone along. This year, my students' spring breaks overlapped. Half of them were last week, and half of them this week. I couldn't afford to take two weeks off lessons, so I stuck around home to have two slower-paced, relaxing weeks of teaching.

Someone tapped on my window. I rolled it down.

"Well you ran out here fast," Tracie said.

"Sorry." I guess I really hadn't spoken to anyone. Oops. "My brain was totally somewhere else."

"Do you have somewhere to be?"

"No. My family abandoned me." I grinned as I said it. Usually I headed over to my parents' place to get one of Mom's solid, home-cooked meals after church.

"That's what I thought. Join us for lunch? We're eating out. Tim, Andrew, Claire, and I decided to invite the visiting couple out. You know, Michael and Amber."

I assumed they were the ones who sat on the back left-hand side, with a baby who was around a year old.

"One of these days I'll get my life together and actually be able to invite people to my *home* on Sundays." She placed a hand on her forehead and shook her head. "Life. But are you coming?"

"Sure." Why not? I didn't have anything else to do. A singleness perk right there.

"Wanna tag along? I can move Emma's booster."

"Oh that's okay, I'll drive. Just text me where exactly we're going so we all end up at the same place." One too many times I'd tried to go out with a group only to end up at the wrong restaurant chain.

"Will do!"

Before I pulled out, I shot a text to Caiden.

Well, my day has taken care of itself. Or Tracie has. Going out to eat with a group.

I was the first one at the restaurant. I triple-checked to be sure I was in the same place Tracie had texted. Convinced I was, I scrolled through social media while I waited. Grace announced that she was expecting her third baby. Addison shared a kissy-face selfie on her timeline. *Girl, you're on your honeymoon, for crying out loud!* I shook my head as soon as I realized I sounded just like Mom, who had a strict opinion about a couple taking their honeymoon unplugged. Another friend shared about her date-night with her husband last night. Wait… Ashley was engaged to Conner? I guess they *had* been seeing each other for seven months now. I commented my congratulations then checked my email.

A text came through from Caiden. I tapped on it.

thumbs up

I raised my eyebrows. Okay, he must be busy.

A car pulled in beside me, and I recognized the new couple from church. Everyone else must be here, finally. I stepped out of my car and waited as we clustered together.

"Tim called and reserved a table." Tracie bounced Emma as the toddler fussed. "I know you're hungry. We're about to get some mac 'n' cheese, okay? Sound good?"

I grinned and followed as we made our way to a table reserved for the size of our group. Chaos reigned for about five minutes as parents made sure their kids got seated and everyone ordered. As soon as the first batch of plates was brought out, everyone hushed, and Tim blessed the food.

"So tell me, Amber," Claire addressed the new girl. "How did you and Michael meet?"

I ate my loaded nachos in silence as the three couples started swapping their love stories. I had heard Andrew and Claire's and Tim and Tracie's a few times now. Bible college for both of them. Married before the age of twenty. Andrew and Claire were going on six years with three kids, Tim and Tracie three years with one kid. Now Michael and Amber were in the mix—they had met at work when they were both twenty-one, got married within a year, and were now celebrating two years with one baby here and another just on the way.

While everyone around this table had been busy marrying and having kids, here I was, the oldest of the group, still single. I had kids all right—like fifty I saw each week. But I sent them home after a half hour lesson to pound out piano pieces away from me. It wasn't the same as raising darlings like these sitting around the table.

Life suddenly seemed to stretch out before me. An endless stream of learning and polishing my own pieces and teaching students. Nothing ever changing. The only thing exciting in my life was when I got coupons for a free chicken sandwich.

I slid my eyes to my phone right under the ledge of the table and typed out, *Help me! I'm drowning in this sea of married people!* My finger hovered over the "send" button, but I stopped. Caiden was in the process of joining their forces and was over-the-top happy about his girl. I selected the text, copied and cut it. But no... I couldn't paste and send it to Livvy. That was all levels of meanness. I swallowed and put my phone aside. There were people here for me to chat with. I'd just wait and join in their conversation as soon as there was something I could identify with.

five

J stared at my phone screen. It was too early to call it a night, so I was lying on my stomach across my bed, scrolling idly through social media. It had been two days. Livvy texted occasionally, but I knew she was hurting. And when she was hurting, she wanted to be alone. So I let her. Caiden, on the other hand... yeah, he totally wasn't hurting. He had sent me a two-screen length text Sunday night. Apparently, he was on a streak of seeing Rachel every day, because here it was, Tuesday night, and from pictures he'd sent me, he'd not missed a day seeing her. When he set his mind on something, he was all in. They were cute together. Adorable, really. And those smiles...

I flopped to my back. The last dozen texts I had sent were to students' parents about lesson schedules this week. Okay, and a few texts with Elise—but she was up in a mountain cabin where cell reception was worse than spotty, which made it frustrating to try to hold a conversation with her. And I just wanted a quick, fun exchange with someone right now. Anyone.

I tossed my phone, and it bounced on the mattress beside me.

Lonely.

That was the word to describe me.

Ugh. God, I don't want *this struggle!* For crying out loud, I was twenty-seven. I had grown through the whole teen-crush stage where each guy was a potential suitor until I came to my senses and realized that he really wasn't. I had passed through my early twenties when all of the friends my age were getting married. Now, the cousins I remembered visiting in the hospital after their births were up and getting married—or into serious relationships. Here I was, knocking on thirty's door, and the only single guys I knew weren't married for very obvious reasons.

I knew how to be flippant about the topic. Man, I had totally aced it with these ten years of practice. For over three thousand, six hundred fifty days, I had deflected thousands of comments.

"Just you wait. You're next."

"You're totally going to be smitten."

"Honey, God has a man for you right around the corner."

"Who's *your* eye on?"

"You went out to eat? Who was he?"

"I know you've got *someone* somewhere."

"Wait… you mean, you aren't dating right now?"

Oh, I could take it from Caiden, Livvy, and my immediate family. They knew I was waiting on God and not just dating any jerk out there in desperation. Their teasing was just that—good-natured, loving teasing.

The problem was... no one had even asked me out. Okay, if you discounted that kid last year who was mortified to find out he didn't even live in the same decade as me.

I wondered... what number wedding would I be on my list? One-sixty-one? Ha... no, because I already had that one scheduled a month from this weekend, and I wasn't going to meet some guy to up and marry by then. Two hundred? That would be in approximately... two years? That'd be acceptable. I wouldn't be thirty quite yet. We'd still have the potential of having three or four kids before I was too old.

Why is it even bothering me tonight?

I picked up my phone again and tapped to text Livvy. My fingers hovered over the screen. What would I say? *Pray for me, I'm struggling with that age-old singleness problem. Again.*

Right. When she was struggling with the pain of a recent break-up. It was hard to not share this trouble with her—to know that *someone* had my back. I could text Caiden. He was a good prayer partner and goodness knows how many times he'd had to listen to my single-girl woes. But that just didn't feel right either. And Elise... she was ten years younger than me. We were just now getting to where we had those deeper sister conversations.

I jumped off my bed. Well, desperate times called for desperate measures. I marched into the kitchen and grabbed the carton of ice cream. Spooned out twice the recommended serving. Melted my chocolate. Drizzled it on top. Stuck the ice cream back in the freezer then padded back to the living room and plopped down on the loveseat with my Bible.

Caiden would totally laugh at the picture I made. He'd call me the "typical old maid." With that easygoing grin of his, I could take practically any jab from him. I almost sent him a picture but stopped. He was taking Rachel to meet his parents. He wouldn't even look at my text until late tonight—probably after I was in bed. Plus, he might have the audacity to bring up the need to solve the double-date "problem."

I turned back to my Bible. I knew exactly where to go. Psalm 37 was always my go-to for… well, anything. The verses calmed me. I had half of them underlined from different readings throughout the years. Tick-marks beside other verses from my younger years, when I was still hesitant about really marking in my Bible.

I read the verses slowly. The gnawing pain in my heart subsided somewhat, and I opened a new note file in my phone. I couldn't text anyone, but I could journal. I sometimes kept track of my thoughts at random times anyway.

Tonight, it struck again. That age-old "I'm still single" issue. Why? I've got a great life. I love my life. I couldn't quite see myself dropping my students. I mean, some of them I totally could. But the others?

I paused and thought about the ones I had taught today—some of my favorites. The ones that had me biting the sides of my cheeks to not laugh at their hilarious sayings. The ones who couldn't quite get the full word "metronome" out, so just lengthened it to "metro-meter." I didn't have the heart to correct them. They'd learn it eventually. Or the one who thrust a piece of lined school paper in my hand filled with notes and hearts and "Your the best techer ever!" Or the student who couldn't remember "major" and "minor" so called them "regular" and "different" chords. I grinned. I had corrected that one, but I totally loved hearing her mix-up.

I turned back to my journal. *Anyway, I've always been the rather stoic, "totally fine being single" girl. But deep inside, underneath my crusty pretense of resistance to marriage, this gal's heart truly does desire it "someday." Except now that I have figured that out, I almost want "someday" to be... well, tomorrow.*

Why did it strike me *now,* when I was least expecting it?

Because that's how life was. Everything would flow smoothly—a harmonious orchestral beauty—when suddenly, half the instruments drop out with a crash, no warning or explanation given, leaving the rest of the instrumentalists in a stupefied daze.

My ice cream was getting melty as I was sitting there. I spooned up the liquid parts first then moved on to the still-frozen sections where the chocolate had hardened into a shell. I'd be better tomorrow. For a spring break day, I had ten students lined out and then choir practice and church service. Putting my focus elsewhere would help me from imploding with this ridiculous problem. It would pass quickly.

Six

*E*xcept it didn't pass quickly. Two weeks went by. I stared at my reflection in the mirror on Monday morning. I wasn't exactly young anymore. There were a few wrinkles in my forehead. I leaned in closer and groaned. Five hairs that *could* be considered gray. Last time I had stopped to look, there were only two. I snaked my fingers through my hair then secured it in a clip.

Was I cute? I frowned at my reflection. Yeah, definitely not cute that way. I grinned, but in my eyes, I could see the hint of struggle. I spun on my heel and left the bathroom. *Vanity, vanity, all is vanity...*

I had almost half an hour before needing to leave for the Christian academy where I taught part-time. Next semester, I was totally scheduling these group music classes for later in the week. Herding a bunch of rambunctious toddlers and giving them an introduction to the music world wasn't exactly my high calling for Monday mornings—I was certain of that. Now, sitting in my studio while I taught piano one-on-one? *That* I could gear myself up for every Monday.

But this paid the bills and it was too late to change schedules now.

I reached for my phone to turn on some music and noticed three texts from Livvy.

When do you think it'll get easier?

I don't have to go to work until this afternoon. I bet you're busy, huh?

Is it a crime to spend my morning shopping? I know I'm stress-shopping. I don't have money for a new wardrobe.

Poor thing. I typed out a quick response.

Yeah, have to visit my wee ones this morning. Pray for me. ;) Patience is already thin and I haven't even started. Shop if you need to. Just send me selfies and stick the dress back on the rack.

A sudden pang darted through me. Last time Liv sent me dress pics, it was THE dress. Heavily beaded, just like Livvy wanted, with butterfly sleeves and a six-foot train. She knew it was "technically too early to be looking," but we had both assumed that Jake would pop the question now that graduation was right around the corner. Plus, she had found an awesome sale that couldn't be passed up.

No longer in the mood for listening to music, I turned to my piano. I often found comfort in playing—even while practicing. I pulled out my binder and flipped through the music for Beth's wedding. She had requested three songs I wasn't familiar with. The wedding was week after next, so I probably needed to get to work on them.

Especially since one was being sung by the groom's brother, and we wouldn't rehearse until the day before the wedding. It was an unwritten law in my book that the pianist was ninety-nine percent responsible for a well-executed piece. If the accompanist wasn't confident, the singer would waver. I'd had that happen to me several times in my early years of playing.

I glanced at my phone as it vibrated.

I can't do it. I got in my car to go shopping, but the only thought in my mind was that I won't have a guy to please with my new wardrobe.

Livvy was probably holding back the tears now. I sighed and texted back. *But you weren't gonna buy anything, right?* I added a winkie face. Sometimes humor helped. I stuck the phone on my music rack and began to sightread the music in front of me. My eyes glanced over the words.

Love... union... answer... love... love... love...

I interrupted the song and grabbed my phone as soon as Livvy texted.

No...

Okay, humor hadn't really helped. Today really wasn't a good day for me to help my hurting friend. My own heart was fighting against its own forbidden longings. I pushed that aside.

So, whatcha going to do this morning?

Her reply came quickly. She must have been waiting.

Dunno. Try not to feel miserable?

I tapped my phone to my chin as I thought and prayed. I wished she had another friend to help her out in this specific area, but most of Livvy's other friends were already divorced at her age. I'd seen the bitterness in some of their faces. They were old before their time. I was glad she wasn't going to them for counsel—she didn't need to adopt the attitude they had.

You could join me at the academy. ;)

Speaking of... I glanced at the time. I'd better leave now if I wanted to be sure traffic didn't make me late. I slipped on my sandals and flung my purse over my shoulder as I stepped out the door.

The song I had just been playing wove through my mind as I drove to the academy. I didn't know the song, so the only part that repeated in my mental soundtrack was, "There is loooove." I could totally hear a country singer crooning it. "There is loooove."

Except when there wasn't. Like... my life.

I was still reading Psalm 37 every night. It was almost my lullaby now. Tonight, I was going to take it a step further though. For crying out loud, it had been over fourteen days, and I still couldn't drown out the yearning in my heart for my own special somebody—a somebody who was either hiding under a rock or maybe didn't even exist. Yeah. I was going to journal what stood out to me today in my present situation. Not just the typical "delight in God, He'll give you the desires of your heart." There were some lessons that just stuck when you learned them. That was one I had learned when I was twenty or twenty-one. The process wasn't to pour out my life to God and *expect* Him to provide what I wanted. No, it was delighting in God so His desires would become my own.

And that was what was throwing me for a loop here. Marriage was God's design. To have a stoic, "single-only" mentality was to degrade the calling God placed upon men and women to marry and raise a Godly seed. My desire was completely Biblical. To marry and have my own kids—even to raise my children in the Lord. I was grateful for this woman's high calling, yet here I was— needing to be content as a single businesswoman and wait on God's timing for this God-given desire.

I came to a red light and pulled out my phone. As expected, Livvy had rejected the offer to accompany me. She made no secret about liking kids only minimally— and only one at a time, not a group. That was where we differed.

The light turned green and I accelerated. I *did* love my kids at the academy. Back in August, they had been a shy, quiet group. The girls had twirled their short khaki skirts, some of them with fingers in their mouths, as I had tried to convince them to use the noisemakers. Now, as soon as I walked in the door, they swarmed me, all trying to get a hug from Miss Blackwell. The boys had to have an almost -screaming contest to give me a quick life-update. I loved it. Even if there *were* days like today when I didn't think I could handle twenty of them at once.

But one or two that age? Phoebe and Kyle, two of the kids at the academy, totally had my heart. I wanted kids just like them one day. She was a year older than him, but they were in the same class. And every week, her little chubby arm wrapped around his shoulders, directing him to follow me. Their blue eyes were wide with attentiveness and awe as I spoke to the group—almost as if it was just me and them in the room. Man. I loved those kids. The ache in my heart grew a little bigger as I pulled into the academy's drive.

Seven

Six o'clock still good for you?

I grinned at Caiden's text as I replied, *Better be. I'm about to walk out the door.*

I had changed from the T-shirt I'd been teaching in all day to a red top. The dark denim skirt I was already wearing worked with it. We weren't going anywhere fancy, but it wasn't fast food, for which I was grateful. That's what Caiden usually suggested. But because Rachel was eating dinner with us, his thrifty ideals had gone to the wash.

Caiden: Okay. We may be a little late. Traffic.

I sent a thumbs' up. It looked like this free, single gal was going to be the first to the restaurant. Again. I glanced at my hair. It had been up in a ponytail all day but had survived decently. My blonde strands liked to hang out loose anyway, whether it was five minutes or five hours after I had fixed it. Maybe I should actually care more about my appearance. Do some layers. Curl my partial-wavy, partial-straight tresses. Psh. That took way too much time.

I walked out to my car. Alone. My heart skipped a beat as I thought for a moment what it would be like to actually have a double date with Caiden and Rachel. Oh, Caiden and I just teased about double dating, but deep inside, I had kinda hoped that we'd actually be able to go through this phase of life together. Instead, once again I had a friend take that step and leave me behind.

I should just get an online dating profile. At least a dozen couples I had played for had met that way, and so far, they were all still married. Or the ones I actually still kept up with. Some clients I only saw once and never got in touch with again.

I stopped and pulled out my phone before I cranked my car. I had to get a grip on my thoughts before they led me astray. I opened the notes app I had started last night and reread the entry I had journaled.

"Wait on the Lord, and keep His way, and He shall exalt you to inherit the land…" Psalm 37:34

In every season of waiting, our impatience will tempt us to DO something. We might begin to wonder where WE need to change or do something differently. And sometimes, maybe we do need to change—but only if changing is in keeping God's ways. Changing because "I've tried God's way and it doesn't work" never yields good fruit. In our waiting, let us never grow weary of keeping God's ways.

Yeah. I wasn't going to go online to look for a husband. Not that I thought it was wrong, but I knew that for *me* the motive was one of desperation—not because I thought God was leading me to go that route.

I put on a background Christian piano playlist and cranked my car. A light drizzle sprayed my windshield. The way the wind was blowing, a good garden rain would be soaking in by the time I got to the restaurant.

I hummed along as I drove, switching my wiper blades to slow, then fast, then slow, as the rain couldn't make up its mind how hard it wanted to fall. By the time I got to the restaurant, it was back to a light drizzle. *Thank You, Lord.* I grabbed my purse and scrambled inside before it could pick up again.

Caiden and Rachel weren't so lucky. Caiden, of course, was ever the gentleman and stopped by the door so Rachel would only get minimally wet, but he came in drenched.

"You know, you're supposed to shower *before* you go out in public," I told him as he shook off the droplets from his arms.

"Funny, Steph." He gave a congenial eye-roll before taking Rachel's hand and leading us to a table.

I glanced down at the menu, my eyes landing on the prices before the description of the dish.

Caiden tapped the top of the menu to get my attention. "I'll cover the meal."

I grinned at him. "That's sweet of you. Thanks." My heart lightened. I was still going to watch the dollar signs, but really, who needed a boyfriend when you had a great cousin who still looked out for you?

"Their baked shrimp is totally amazing," Caiden said.

My eyes darted until they found it. "It has—" I stopped mid-sentence when I realized Rachel was talking.

"I've never had shrimp baked. Usually boiled or fried. Is it just as good?"

Caiden wasn't speaking to me. He was speaking to her.

I bit my tongue, hoping Rachel didn't notice we'd talked on top of each other. A weird feeling gnawed itself into my heart. Jealousy? *Jealousy!* Over my cousin? The thought was insane, but the feeling totally wasn't.

Why this jealousy? Just a minute ago, his actions had totally warmed my heart. But now… was it because he was focusing his attention on someone besides me?

Ever since we had called a truce when I was fourteen and he was ten, we'd pretty much been best buds. Sure, we had gone through rocky times after that truce—we never actually hated each other, but there were times we sure weren't happy with the other person. All that history had only brought us closer together. But now things were about to change. Permanently.

I looked at my menu, my eyes not really reading what was there. I was happy for him. I really was. But while he didn't even realize a transition was happening, I was here on the sidelines, watching it take place.

"What would you like to drink?"

I glanced up at the waitress. "Water with lemon."

"Dr Pepper." Yeah, that was Caiden. Always.

"Water with lemon," Rachel said.

I grinned at her. Just another reason to mark her on my "approval" list. Not that I didn't already approve. First off,

Caiden liked her. I trusted his judgment. Then, I had already met her several times. She was opposite Caiden's boisterous joviality, which was probably exactly what he needed.

"What about the names Stone and Forest?"

I tried to keep my eyebrows from rising as Caiden addressed Rachel. Names? Already? They were moving super fast. Well... I guess not, if they had been attending the same Bible study for almost two years. Still...

Rachel gave Caiden a grin. "I'd consider those names. What about you, Stephanie?" She gave me an almost-shy smile, her voice soft and musical. I bet she had an excellent singing voice. "Are you into trendy names or traditional?"

It made me feel good, having her purposefully include me in their conversation, even though I was technically a third-wheel here. "I like names with solid meanings behind them. I mean, Stephanie means 'crown' and Lynn means 'ruddy-complexioned.' So I'm a ruddy-complexioned crown?" I laughed at myself. "Of course, Caiden James means 'fighting supplanter.'"

"See?" Caiden insert. "All the more reason to name kids something that you *know* what it means. Who can confuse Stone and Forest?"

"Yeah, you're going to raise a nature-named kid in the city?" We had discussed this often. It was on the tip of my tongue to add, "Just don't name one of your kids River. I could never take a nephew with such a wishy-washy name." But then... maybe Rachel liked these names. And I didn't want to offend her.

"I wouldn't want my child to be teased because of their name, though," Rachel said. "My initials spell RAW. Even though it's not that bad, it really hurt me when kids would tease me about it when I was younger."

There was a quip on my tongue that sometimes the rawness never wore off, but I caught myself in time. Instead, I said, "My initials are SLB. Nothing creative." It was a stilted save, but safe.

The conversation shifted gears as our food came, and I breathed slightly easier. However, for most of the evening, I was unsettled about whether I should join the conversation or sit back and listen, since they were conversing just fine without me. My relationship with Caiden just got tons more complicated with another girl in the mix.

Eight

God... This. Is. So. Hard! Rain dumped in streams as I sat in my driveway. For the first time in years, I couldn't say that I'd enjoyed my time out with Caiden. But then, it wasn't just time with Caiden. It was Caiden and Rachel. *Why can't I just be excited for him and not feel sorry for myself?* I gritted my teeth and let the rain do the crying for me. I was totally not going to cry over this. *Selfish brat.*

This was it. I needed some reinforcement. I was going to text Livvy. But when I pulled out my phone, there was a text from her waiting.

I just saw Jake's mom at the store. What should I do?

Oh boy. I swallowed back my own struggle and replied, *It's going to be okay. Just smile and be nice to her.*

Livvy: Okay... I mean, like, I totally just hid three aisles down. Should I back up and find her?

I grinned. Dear, over-thinking Livvy.

Me: I don't think that will be necessary. But don't try to avoid her all night. If you see her again, then be sweet.

I added a winkie face to hopefully add a touch of humor to my words.

Livvy: Okay...

Lightning flashed. I probably should go inside and not risk being fried in my vehicle. I had to grin when I realized that being fried would eliminate all of life's problems rather quickly. Still smiling, I glanced around my car for an umbrella. Yeah. Just like I figured. I had left it inside my house by the front door. Oh well, there wasn't anyone home to worry about whether or not I was wet.

I leaned back and watched the rain drizzle down my windshield for another minute. I wasn't ready to go inside yet, and it had nothing to do with the rain. I didn't necessarily want a husband to be home for me every evening. I mean, I kinda did. But it would also be fine to just have a guy that I could text any moment of any day. I could sit here and send him marooned-in-my-car-in-a-deluge selfies. Like I used to do with Caiden, until recently.

Ugh! I jammed my phone into my purse, grabbed my box of leftovers, got my house key ready to go, then made a run for the front door. My small place was quiet and dark. I turned on all the lights. Lit a few candles. Put music on full blast. Anything to chase away the gloomy, lonesome shadows that now haunted the corners.

I plopped down on the loveseat and looked at the empty cushion beside me. Why did I even have a loveseat?

"For *crying* out loud!" I turned and perched my legs across the other cushion. There. It was full. I opened my

Bible app and selected Psalm 37. I read through each verse slowly, latching my attention onto it as if it were a new passage of music I was trying to learn under pressure.

Verse sixteen stopped me. "A little that a righteous man hath is better than the riches of many wicked."

I mulled over the words. There was something there for me. I copied the verse to my notes and typed out, *A little.* I paused to think, then my fingers flew. *It is easy to focus on the little that we have as singles. A little income. A little of our own space. Not to mention the complete absence of some things, such as a husband or children. But... if we are righteous in what we are doing, then the little that we have is better than the increase of the wicked. Other girls may have guys hanging on their arms. Other girls may have babies. But not every girl has obtained them in righteousness. We should not let the increase of others discourage us in our quest for righteousness.*

Wow. Sometimes I wondered where all these thoughts came from. Because just a few minutes ago, I was totally mourning over my lack. Just because I wrote this down, though, didn't mean I had mastered the message. But... I reread my thoughts. It was comforting.

I kept reading. I wasn't about to go to bed. At this point, I would just fall back into my morose ponderings.

"Mark the perfect man, and behold the upright: for the end of that man is peace." Psalm 37:37. My heart clung to the last part: "the end of that man is peace." I copied it down as well then added, *Ah, how we long for peace. We may not know this is what we're after, but what is it? We don't like the sense of just hanging in limbo, of not knowing, and of feeling that unrest in our hearts. Peace. That is the root of our desire, truly. Seek more of Christ in you... and He will not only enable you to walk upright, but will also give that peace you're longing for.*

That was definitely what I needed tonight. My peace of mind had been completely destroyed, but I was going to regain it, by God's help. I turned off my phone screen and closed my eyes. Since I was alone, I prayed aloud, "Thank You, Lord, for these timely verses. Today, I choose to trust in You and go to You with my trouble. I know that You want what's best for me. You say, 'No good thing will He withhold...'" My eyes flew open and I gave a sheepish grin as I opened my Bible app again and searched those words. Psalm 84:11 was the verse I was thinking of. "...No good thing will He withhold from them that walk uprightly." Years ago, before Livvy and Jake were together, Liv had practically lived on this verse.

"If it's good for me to have a husband then You'll provide him. Just help me to focus on the uprightly part, because I'm totally faltering right now." I didn't close the prayer, because I knew I'd be talking to God again before the night was over.

I wondered if Livvy remembered this verse right now. I opened my phone and shot her a text. *Psalm 84:11.* That's all I said, but it was enough. She'd look it up and would take it from there. And God would help her to glean whatever encouragement she needed from it.

For now, I needed to grab a shower and hopefully, by then, my heart would be calm enough to go to bed.

Tomorrow was a long day with teaching and Wednesday night church services. First though, I copied out Psalm 37:37 and taped it to my shower wall. If I set my mind to memorizing it, maybe I would have less time to dwell on singleness and struggles.

Nine

Ten days until the next wedding. It was that realization *only* that made me pull out my black binder and tackle those love songs. Thankfully, after this, I didn't have a wedding lined up for several months. I could do this.

My fingers flew over the keys as I ran through a few scales. I played a quick Chopin piece by memory. Just to get my brain from teaching to practice mode. Or so I pretended. I really knew that I was just procrastinating. Delaying the inevitable. My alarm rang. I had to leave for church in half an hour to be early enough for choir practice. Okay, better get this over with. I flipped open to a piece I hadn't looked at yet. For this one, I was accompanying a violinist. As long as she was confident in the melody, it would go smoothly with just a few minutes' rehearsal. It wasn't anything major like a processional where we'd have to figure out when to stop or go back to accommodate the attendants. I tripped over the notes as I got a feel for the rhythm and melody. First run-throughs were always pretty pathetic, and this was no different. I came to the cadence and let the notes fade into silence. Now that I had a fair idea of how it went, I played it again. This time, the lyrics taunted me. All about love. The one and only. A lifetime of dreams. Promises. Cherishing. Fulfilled longings.

Ugh!

I stopped mid-chord and flattened my hands on the keys. It wasn't banging. I hadn't really banged on the piano in anger since my immature teen years. But this subtle blob of discordant notes had the same effect—my frustration in sound. And it wasn't a melodic sound. I quickly moved my fingers to play an F major chord, long and flowing. Closing my eyes, my right hand picked out a melody.

'Tis so sweet to trust in Jesus.

I stopped and glared at my hands. That wasn't exactly the song I had on my heart, even if it was one of my favorites. But I started it again, this time, playing the full verse. The song would spin in my head unless I actually played it to the end.

> 'Tis so sweet to trust in Jesus.
> Just to take Him at His Word;
> Just to rest upon His promise,
> Just to know, "Thus saith the Lord!"

I paused before I played the chorus. I should do my own arrangement of this one. It had been several months since I had taken the time to create my own rendition of a hymn. I had no excuse today. I could totally finish learning that love song next week. I closed my eyes and let my fingers play around on the keys. An introduction formed—a play on the melody, as if teasing the listener to start singing along before it was time. I jotted down a few notes to remember it next time I sat down at the piano then grabbed the hymnal from the shelf beside me. That was one downfall of being a pianist—I didn't actually know all these words by heart, even though I'd played the hymn a good hundred times. I usually read notes and just enough words to catch a glimpse of the context. This time, I slowed to actually read the lyrics as I played.

> Oh, how sweet to trust in Jesus,
> Just to trust His cleansing blood;
> Just in simple faith to plunge me
> 'Neath the healing, cleansing flood!
>
> Yes, 'tis sweet to trust in Jesus,
> Just from sin and self to cease;
> Just from Jesus simply taking
> Life and rest and joy and peace.
>
> I'm so glad I learned to trust Thee,
> Precious Jesus, Savior, Friend;
> And I know that Thou art with me,
> Wilt be with me to the end.
>
> *Jesus, Jesus, how I trust Him!*
> *How I've proved Him o'er and o'er;*

Jesus, Jesus, precious Jesus!
Oh, for grace to trust Him more!

Wow. I knew that this was a beautiful piece, but today, it was the cry of my heart. Trusting God at His Word—was that not what I was attempting to do with my focus on Psalm 37 lately? Trusting His cleansing blood… that phrase made me stop. If I could trust Jesus with holding my salvation, how much more could I trust Him with holding my future?

Life and rest and joy and peace. That reminded me of the verse I had worked on memorizing last night. "The end of that man is peace." And then the last verse: I'm so glad I learned to trust Thee.

The book of James mentions how the trying of our faith works patience and patience hope. I wasn't naive. I knew that this life would be full of trials. But sometimes, when they took me by surprise—such as this sudden struggle with singleness—I forgot.

Then finally, "Wilt be with me to the end." Jesus knew what *my* end would be. He knew how long I was going to be single—or if I would ever marry. The beauty of it was that, whether married or single, He was with me. He'd never leave me nor forsake me. He didn't even gauge my worth by my marital status. He loved me the same, regardless.

And it was because of all those promises that I could trust Him. I read the lyrics again, thinking through the word painting I could do in an arrangement—how could I make the piano sing in such a way that the listeners would reflect on the lyrics that weren't being verbalized?

You know what, this would be a good song for Livvy right now. She had sent back a row of hearts to my verse last night, and today we had chatted back and forth a little. I picked up my phone to copy the lyrics down for her and my gaze fell on the time.

Oh my goodness! I should have left for church five minutes ago! I flicked off the lights and ran out the door. Well, this was a good way to forget my struggles for the moment. By the way my heart was racing, though, I wasn't going to make a regular habit of it.

Ten

*I*t was Friday. I sat back in my chair as I listened to ten-year-old Kate play her piece. She was whispering the timing under her breath, and her fingers moved mechanically. At the sixth measure, she hit a wrong note and stopped. "Let me start over."

"See if you can keep going," I encouraged. I pointed to the note she had missed. "What's this?"

She played two wrong notes before hitting the right one. Her face drew tight in concentration, and she continued to the end of the piece.

"There you go! You didn't have to start over—you just figured out what was wrong in that one place, then you had it." I continued talking, discussing the style of the piece, certain techniques she could use to make the piece sound more like music and less like a slew of notes strung together. My phone buzzed, and I glanced down at it. "And… there we have it." Her half hour was up. Time for lunch.

I waited until she was out the door before I opened my text app. Livvy had messaged earlier, but I tried to avoid texting during lessons unless something was an emergency. This? I had glanced at the preview earlier and, it assured me it wasn't an emergency. Now I read the text in full.

Livvy: You free this evening? Want to eat supper together? Your place?

I grinned. A friend wasn't a true friend unless they could invite themselves over. *Sure. My last lesson ends at 6:00. Pizza?*

She sent an emoji of clapping hands. I went to pull out sandwich fixings for lunch and checked to be sure I actually *had* the ingredients for pizza. It wasn't something I made unless there was someone to share it with, which wasn't as often as I liked.

A twinge of loneliness darted through me and I pushed it away. The irony of what I had just told Kate struck me. You couldn't start over. You had to stop, learn the solution, and keep going. *No good thing will He withhold...* The feeling didn't go away, so I pulled out my phone and let it read Psalm 37 aloud to me as I dug in the pantry and fridge, fixed my lunch, and started eating.

"...He is their strength in time of trouble."

I opened the app to see which verse it was on. "But the salvation of the righteous is of the Lord: He is their strength in the time of trouble." Psalm 37:39. I paused the audio and reflected on that verse. Copied it. Pasted it to my growing notes file. I set my sandwich down and brushed the crumbs off my fingers so I could type.

This last phrase... God, our strength in time of trouble. As singles, we surely are not exempt from troubles! Often, though, we're tempted to wish for a husband just so we'd have a comforting "arm of flesh" to lean on—or so that we would not have to make all the decisions. It takes strength to keep going alone... but are we truly alone? We should not even think that way, because God is our strength! Whatever the trouble we face, He is stronger. And He is there to support us.

That was it! The root of my problem. I wanted a fleshly arm to lean on. These last few weeks, when I usually would've turned to Caiden or Livvy for a listening ear, I couldn't. I had to actually turn to God alone, and I wasn't used to that. Wow.

I reached for my sandwich and took another bite, slowly chewing it. I guess I'd never truly relied on God alone. His Word alone. Oh, I thought I had. But how often when I needed prayer did I shoot a text to someone else and *then* remember that I actually should pray too? Now that I was more or less forced to be on my own, I realized just how much I leaned on others. And that was one of the driving forces behind me wanting my own guy—a temporal security that he would always be there for me. That he would be *my* special friend.

Someone knocked on my door, and I downed a gulp of water. I had forgotten I had rescheduled Brandon to come now instead of at 5:30. I pushed my thoughts back and focused once more on piano and my students.

That evening, I pulled out flour, oil, and yeast as soon as my last student walked out the door—at 5:30, not 6:00.

Oh well. I turned the music on to something I could sing along with as I mixed up pizza crust. I'd just have them ready for toppings by the time Livvy got here.

It was right at 6:00 when she knocked and let herself in.

"Wow, when did punctuality become your strong point?"

Livvy dropped her purse by the door and skipped over to me. "It's working out, Steph!"

My heart sped up. "*It...?*" I didn't want to guess Jake, but that's what I was hoping.

"You sent me that verse and then the song this week, and they were just so encouraging. I set aside some serious time to seek God and just pray—pray for Jake, his family, our relationship, God's will and direction. Yesterday, Jake called and said he'd had a long talk with his parents. They worked out so many things, and he thinks it's time to talk again. *They're* okay with it. Even encouraged it. And by then, God had worked in my heart—really worked in my heart—about moving so far away..." Tears were sliding down her face as she wrapped me in a hug.

I hugged her back awkwardly, my hands full of olive juice from the pizzas. "I'm really, *really* glad for you, Liv. This is such an answer to prayer!" I laughed and apologized for my awkwardness, and she brushed it off. And just like that, the silence of the last few weeks was erased, and I had my chattering, excited, bubbly friend back. She didn't stay late—with a guilty grin, she admitted that she had planned to see a movie with Jake, but wanted to visit me first, and this was the only excuse she could make. So by 7:30, my house was again empty, my best friend reconnecting with her boyfriend.

I glanced around the messy kitchen that I had insisted Livvy leave for me to clean. "Well," I said to the silence. "Everything worked out quickly for her." And I didn't feel a hint of jealousy as I said it. She sought God, He answered. But that wasn't how it always worked. In the Bible, Joseph had faced two years of silence after everything worked out well for the butler. And the timing was perfect. He was where he needed to be, doing what he needed to do, when he needed to do it.

Forget the kitchen. I slipped onto the piano bench and played through "'Tis so Sweet to Trust in Jesus." I had made progress in my arrangement yesterday and only had the last verse to finish. The one that rang of surety in the fact that it *is* sweet to trust in Jesus. It needed a key change—something higher, more emphatic, more movement. My heart sang as my fingers played. Because the message was sinking in. It *was* sweet to trust in Jesus.

When I finally left my piano to clean the kitchen, I grabbed my phone to turn on music. A text from Caiden was waiting.

How much do you charge for a wedding?

My heart skipped a beat—I'm sure of it. My fingers flew. *Why...?*

Caiden: Oh, you know, just in case Rachel wants you to play for our wedding...

I called him. He answered with a serious, business-type voice. "Hello?"

"Wedding talk? For real?"

I could almost hear him rolling his eyes as he said, "It's not like we've only known each other a month."

"True. But—well—have you asked her?" As I asked, I realized that I wanted him to be serious. If God was leading him to take this next step, I was ready for it too.

"Eh…" He tried to sound nonchalant, but I could hear the pent-up excitement thrumming through him.

"You're about to?!" I pushed the phone against my ear, not wanting to miss even a mutter.

Finally, Caiden laughed. "Don't worry. I'm not gonna rush into things."

"Don't you dare do anything without telling me first." I almost felt bad, half-threatening him. But, he was my cousin. One of my best friends.

Caiden laughed again. "You'll be the first to know. I *promise.*"

Epilogue

Four Months Later

*M*usic filtered from the auditorium then stopped. I glanced at Livvy, who was looking over her shoulder as the photographer snapped a picture. She was in the dress that, just a few short months ago, she had bemoaned the possibility of never wearing. I grinned at the memory.

The music started again. I listened as the opening of the Bridal Chorus began. Then stopped.

"I'll be right back, Liv." A mulberry-purple puddle of chiffon formed around my bare feet as I stood, but I refused to put on heels before I absolutely had to. I grabbed the excess fabric and held it high enough to keep me from tripping as I entered the empty auditorium.

"Hey," I said.

Tiffany looked at me glumly. She was one of my senior students and had been playing piano only six years, but her dedication had brought her to the top of my studio.

There was no one better I could think of entrusting to play for my best friend's wedding—since she insisted I couldn't get away from being her maid of honor.

"You can do this!" I encouraged. "Trust me. It sounded great and you didn't have to stop."

She shook her hands before placing them on the keys. "What if I mess up her entire bridal chorus? Her wedding?"

I gave her a gentle smile. "I used to worry about that at every single wedding."

Tiffany rolled her eyes. "Yeah, but you're phenomenal. You didn't even have to worry."

I laughed as I stopped beside the piano. "Trust me, I have had my fair share of completely *un*-phenomenal mishaps. And you know what? I'm still quite alive today." I leaned forward and whispered, "Wanna know the truth? I'd rather be in your shoes than mine." Well, except I didn't have shoes on. But that was beside the point.

"Really?"

"Yeah. I'm comfortable playing. This?" I shifted and the purple shimmered with every movement. "I don't know how to do 'fancy' very well, but I'll do it for my best friend. And you'll do just fine. I'm praying for you!"

She took a deep breath, and I could see the tension relaxing.

"Now," I said, "you know your music perfectly. One hour before the wedding isn't going to change anything. Step away from the piano and find something to relax you."

"All right."

I gave her another grin before stepping down the steps. My foot caught on the hem of my gown and I stumbled three feet forward before righting myself. I glanced over my shoulder. "Just watch me fall, and *no one* will be paying attention to the piano music!"

Tiffany laughed, and I sensed that most of her nerves were dissipating. I still breathed a quick prayer for her before leaving the auditorium and entering the foyer.

"Quick! Jake's driving up! You can't let him see her!"

Livvy's mom pushed me toward the bride. I grabbed Livvy's hand and we hurried down the hall and into the back room. I slammed the door and leaned against it. "There. Safe."

Livvy sank into the cushioned chair and let out a half-laugh, half-sigh. "Oh Steph... it's been so wonderful! I'm going to miss you *so* much!" She started blinking quickly.

"Nuh-uh..." I held out my finger to her and frowned. "No tears." I refused to think about her moving so many miles away and instead focused on the positive. God *had* worked things out so beautifully for her and Jake. In His perfect timing. And today I was going to witness my best friend and her fiancé become wife and husband.

Someone tapped on the door and Livvy's eyes widened. I placed my hand on the knob and called out, "Who's there?"

"Hey, Steph, it's me."

Caiden.

"You can't see the bride."

"I'm not wanting to."

I glanced back at Livvy and she shrugged. I slipped out.

"I want to show you *so* bad, but Rachel would kill me if she knew I did!"

"Uh… explanation?"

Caiden ran his fingers through his hair and unsuccessfully tried to bite back a smile. "The ring."

"The *ring?*" I lowered my voice and leaned forward. "You're really asking her?" He had constantly talked about it, kept hinting at it, but always said, "Soon."

A wide grin broke out on his face. "Today, after the wedding. But I can't show you the ring. I *want* to."

"Don't you dare," I warned. "I won't look at it. Rachel needs to be the first to see it." And here I was, sounding like Mom again.

Caiden suddenly reached forward and pulled me into a hug. "I'm just so excited!"

I smiled as I squeezed him back. There was absolutely no doubt in my mind but that Rachel would say yes. "I'm excited for you, too." And I truly was. God had done an amazing work in my heart and I was ready to let Caiden move on with Rachel as his best friend.

"I need to let you get back to… brides… maiding… or whatever…"

I laughed and swatted him gently. "Thanks. Send me pictures as soon as you can, though, or I'll be on your doorstep."

He grinned again—actually, he had never really stopped grinning.

"You might want to look normal or she's gonna suspect something."

Caiden shrugged. "I don't care." He waved as he literally bounced back down the hall where guests were starting to gather.

I slipped back in the room and glanced at my watch. "Forty minutes!"

Livvy gave an excited squeal then instantly sobered. "But I'm just so sad to be leaving, you know. I won't be here when you find your guy and—"

I stopped her with a laugh. "Trust me, hon, you'll definitely hear whenever a guy happens to come around for me." I knelt on the floor beside her. "But I don't wager it will be anytime soon."

"Steph, your dress."

I shrugged my shoulders. "It won't hurt anything." I reached under her chair—the perfect hiding place—and pulled out a wrapped box. "This is for you."

She raised her eyebrows. "But you already gave me my wedding gift."

"That was your engagement gift. This is your *wedding* gift. Open it!"

She snapped the tape and gently folded the paper away from the box. I knew what the gift was, but I still leaned forward to get another glimpse of it.

"Oh… Stephanie!" Livvy blinked wildly.

"You're gonna run mascara."

She crushed me in a hug.

"And wrinkle your dress."

"Stop it."

I gave a satisfied sigh and hugged my friend, squeezing my eyes shut against my own tears. When she finally released me, I placed my hand on the wooden sign she had opened.

"God is faithful Who promises," I said, giving her a smile that felt wobbly.

"He sure is."

Her slender fingers traced the white letters.

> *"No good thing will He withhold*
> *from them that walk uprightly."*
> Psalm 84:11

I echoed the words in my mind. God absolutely knew what was best for me and yes, it *was* so sweet to trust in Jesus and take Him at His Word.

Author's Note

I am half-tempted to give Stephanie more in her epilogue. In a story like this, we want to hear when she *did* get married. But when it comes to us single gals, the future is just unsure. We might meet a guy the next year, we might be forty or fifty years old, or God might call us to a lifetime of singleness. It is more realistic to let Steph's story dangle unfinished and have her learn contentment without the realization of her dreams.

If I claimed that this doesn't hint at being auto-biographical, I would lie. At the time of writing this, I am 28 and single. I have adopted Steph's attitude of taking every playful jab at my singleness with good humor. And, for the most part, I am totally fine with being single. But there are days in which I do struggle. Days in which I wonder why God allows some people to marry at a young age, but others He allows to wait. And then I realize that He allows some of us to stay single so we can teach others (I can't say how many times I've thought, "People write all these books on courtship and dating—but *nothing* is written for the siblings left behind!"). If I had been married for eight years and then had written this story…

well, first of all, I wouldn't *personally* know what it's like to go through a season of struggling. Second of all, those reading it would say, "Yeah, easy for her to say, she found her guy when she was young." I'm there with you, friend.

The Psalm 37 notes are directly from my journal in a season when I was struggling a lot with singleness. If you're going through this struggle (or any struggle, for that matter), I highly recommend reading Psalm 37 each night. It helps.

Contentment and waiting on the Lord are lessons for us to continually learn. But it *is* possible to be happily and joyfully single. It doesn't mean we'll never struggle. Like Steph, I've had seasons where all of a sudden, loneliness and discontentment struck me with absolutely no "logic" behind it. But each of these seasons have helped build my trust in the Lord and drawn me closer to His side. Keep turning to the Lord in this season of your life, and He will enrich your life with blessings far above all you could ask or think!

Special Thanks

No book is written alone. Every time I write something, I am overwhelmed with the amazing support group God has given me. So special thanks to...

My married siblings and friends: you'll never know how much your relationships have taught me about singleness.

Rachel: for making me put Livvy through a breakup and helping me decide that it didn't need to be for anything negative, but just that they needed to be separated for a while.

Those who helped me with names: Anita, Jennifer N., Jennifer C., Naomi, Josi, Vicki, Kellyn, Abby, Katja, Grace, and Sage. Thank you for loading me down with more than enough name suggestions! Many of them popped up in the story.

Beau, Rachel and Anita: thanks for late-night conferences on the cover design. Your input made the cover!

Mom: once again, you caught way too many "Amanda-isms" in the manuscript and made it understandable to the world. Thank you!

My beta readers: not only did you help me with the flow of this story, you let me know that the message of this book *would* help single girls. Knowing that before this story hit the shelves has encouraged me more than you know.

My Lord and Savior Jesus Christ: this story wouldn't be here without You. Thank You for putting me in times of struggle. I know You have a perfect reason for it all—and I can't help but wonder if this story is one of those specific reasons for the struggles I've faced as a single. Thank You.

Amanda Tero

Connect with Amanda

Email: amandaterobooks@gmail.com
Website: www.amandatero.com
Facebook: www.facebook.com/amandateroauthor
Instagram: amandateroauthor
Pinterest: amandaruthtero
Blog: www.withajoyfulnoise.blogspot.com
Goodreads: AmandaTero

Amanda Tero began her love for words at a young age—reading anything she could get her hands on and penning short stories as young as age eight. Since graduation, she has honed her writing skills by dedicated practice and study of the writing craft. She began her journey of publication with a few short stories that she had written for her sisters and continued to add to her collection with other short stories, novellas, and novels. It is her utmost desire to write that which not only pleases her Lord and Savior, but also draws the reader into a deeper relationship with Jesus Christ.

More by Amanda Tero

Short Stories
Coffee Cake Days
Finding Christmas Joy
Hartly Manor
Letter of Love
(short story sequel to "Journey to Love")
Letters from a Scatter-Brained Sister
Maggie's Hope Chest
Noelle's Gift
Peace, Be Still
Quest for Leviathan

Novellas
Journey to Love
Wedding Score

Tales of Faith Series
Befriending the Beast
The Secret Slipper
Protecting the Poor

Non-Fiction
Me? Teach Piano?

HAVE YOU MET THE MASTER AUTHOR?

The "author and finisher of our faith," the "author of salvation?"

Well, why do we need to know the Master Author?

There is no man, woman, boy, or girl who is without sin. Romans 3:23 says, "For **all** have sinned, and come short of the glory of God;"

Have you lied, cheated, stolen, taken God's Name in vain, coveted, or lusted? All of these are sins according to God's Holy law (see Exodus 20). Even if we neglect in just one area of God's law, we are found sinners. "For whosoever shall keep the whole law, and yet offend in one point, he is guilty of all." (James 2:10) The payment for sin is death ("For the wages of sin is death;" Romans 6:23a)

God does not desire to leave us in this hopeless, destitute state. He did what we could not do and paid the debt for us. He sent His Son, Jesus Christ, to come, be born of a virgin, live a sinless, perfect life, die a cruel death, and rise again, victorious over sin, death, and hell! Romans 6:23 continues to say, "but the gift of God is eternal life through Jesus Christ our Lord." Jesus Christ is the only way to have eternal life, to be forgiven ("Jesus saith unto him, I am the way, the truth, and the life: no man cometh unto the Father, but by me." John 14:6). God promised us that, "If we confess our sins, He is faithful and just to forgive us our sins, and to cleanse us from all unrighteousness." (1 John 1:9)

Salvation comes by putting your faith and trust in Jesus Christ for salvation and eternity ("Believe on the Lord Jesus Christ, and thou shalt be saved, " Acts 16:31) and repenting from our sins ("Repent ye therefore, and be converted, that your sins may be blotted out," Acts 3:19).

So, have you met the Author?